When Oscar Was a Little Grouch

and Other Good-Night Stories

By Liza Alexander
Illustrated by Tom Brannon

A GOLDEN BOOK • NEW YORK

Published by Golden Books Publishing Company, Inc., in cooperation
with Children's Television Workshop

WHEN OSCAR
WAS A LITTLE GROUCH

One day Oscar was grouch-sitting for his niece Filthomena. She
was just a little slip of a grouch, no bigger than a wastepaper basket.
Today Filthie was giggling and smiling and chatting. "This is
terrible!" thought Oscar. "She's too perky! What would her mother
say? I've got to do something to make her grouchy, and quick!"

Oscar disappeared down into his can and came back up with a
pair of cymbals. *Clang! Clang! Clang!* He crashed them loudly in
Filthie's ear. "Whaaaaaa!" yelled the little Grouch. "What noisy
cymbals, Uncle Oscar! Where did you get them?"

"Well, little Filthie," said Oscar, "when I was your age, my
mother used to say, 'Sleep grumpy, little grouch!' Then she'd play a
grouch lullaby on these cymbals. They make a nice soothing racket,
don't they?"

"They sure do," said Filthie. "Uncle Oscar, what was it like when
you were little?"

"Funny that you should ask!" said Oscar. "I was just going through a few things I've saved from when I was an itty-bitty grouch."

Oscar ducked down into his can once again and popped back up with a chipped spoon and a battered bowl. "My mother fed me my first grouch food with this bowl and spoon. She'd say, 'Eat! It'll make you big and grouchy!'"

"Tell me more, Uncle Oscar, tell me more!" said Filthie.

"Let's see!" Oscar brought out a tiny metal trash can from his own bigger can. "This was my first real trash can. I wore it to kindergrouchen. See how battered and smashed it is! Heh, heh!"

"That can's really awful," said Filthomena. "I wish I had one just like it!"

Bang! Crash! Clank! Oscar rummaged around in his can and pulled out a bashed-up plastic flamingo and a dented toaster. "I got this junk on my very first trip to the dump," he said. "I remember it well. Uncle Oswaldo let me ride in the back of his garbage truck. It was pouring rain, and mud spattered up all over me. It was wonderful!"

"Uncle Oscar, Uncle Oscar! Will you take me to the dump sometime?" asked Filthomena.

"You bet, Filthie," said Oscar. "Anytime!"

Filthomena was so excited that she pouted furiously. She began to fuss and fret and yell. Uncle Oscar joined right in, and they had a high old grumpy time.

Filthie had really worked herself up into a fantastic fit when her mother came stomping around the corner. She gathered her little grouch up in her arms and gave her a big kiss. "Darling!" said Filthomena's mother. "Uncle Oscar must be a great grouch-sitter. I've never seen you in such a great grumpy mood. How did you do it, Oscar?"

"Shucks," said Oscar, "it was nothing!"

TINA TWIDDLEBUG'S
BIG ADVENTURE

One day Thaddeus Twiddlebug, mayor of Twiddlebug Town, said, "It is time that we build a playground for our little Twiddlebugs.

Everybody agreed, and since Twiddlebugs don't like to waste time, they got right to work. Tilly and Titus Twiddlebug used two safety pins and a toothpick to build a frame for a swing set. Then they hung buttons from string to make swings. Tessy Twiddlebug filled a matchbox with sand to make a sandbox, and Toby Twiddlebug stuck a ruler on a thimble for a seesaw.

"Marvelous, marvelous, marvelous!" said the mayor. "This playground is almost complete!"

"Just a minute!" said Tina Twiddlebug. "My Timmy loves to scramble and climb! We must have a jungle gym for our little Twiddlebugs!" Everybody agreed, but nobody could think of what would make a good jungle gym.

Tina took a deep breath and spoke up once again. "I will fly out into the big wide world and find a jungle gym for my Timmy and all the other little Twiddlebugs of our town!"

There was a hush in the crowd as all twiddling stopped. Very few Twiddlebugs had ever ventured out into the big wide world. But Mayor Thaddeus Twiddlebug was all for it. He said, "Here, here!" and clapped Tina on the back.

All the other Twiddlebugs hugged her and wished her good luck. Brave Tina gave her Timmy a big kiss and took off on her tiny Twiddlebug wings into the big wide world.

To Twiddlebugs the big wide world is any place beyond Twiddlebug Town, which is in Elmo's windowbox. And the first place next to Elmo's windowbox is Elmo's bedroom. So when Tina twiddled in through the window, Elmo was sitting on the floor playing a game of jacks.

Elmo was concentrating on his game and didn't notice Tina. And that was a good thing, because even though Elmo is a friendly little monster, Elmo seemed very big and scary to Tina. Ever so quietly Tina began to look for a jungle gym. She twiddled softly around the room.

"Elmo's checkers and his tiddlywinks would make good tables, but not good jungle gyms. His comb would make a fine fence and his dice would make nice chairs. But none of these things would be much fun to climb on. What am I to do?" wondered Tina.

Just then Elmo gave his jacks an extra big toss and one jack
skittered all the way across the floor. Elmo got up and looked for it,
but he couldn't find that jack anywhere. "Oh, well!" he said. "I've
got plenty more jacks." The fuzzy red monster went back to his
game.

But Tina, with her sharp Twiddlebug eyes, knew just where that
jack had gone. She was still a little bit frightened, but when Tina
Twiddlebug makes up her mind, there's no stopping her!

Tina twiddled right down behind the dresser and snatched the
jack up. "It's perfect!" she thought. Off she flew, up from behind the
bureau and out Elmo's window, just as fast as her tiny Twiddlebug
wings could carry her.

Back in Elmo's windowbox, snug in their town, all the other Twiddlebugs waited with their fingers crossed for Tina to come back. When she did, with the jungle jack, all the Twiddlebugs sang and twiddled for joy!

"Tina," said Mayor Thaddeus Twiddlebug, "you make us proud to be Twiddlebugs!" He named her a hero and hung a bright, shiny medal around her neck.

Elmo has never figured out where that jack went, but you can be sure that to this day, thanks to Tina Twiddlebug (and Elmo), the children of Twiddlebug Town scramble and climb to their hearts' content on their very own jungle jack in their very own playground.

GOOD NIGHT, BERT!

"Ooohwee!" sighed Bert. "Am I tuckered out! This old bed of mine is looking mighty inviting." Bert stretched and yawned sleepily. "Yessiree, I sure am looking forward to a little shut-eye."

"Yeah, Bert," said Ernie dreamily. "Uh, Bert? What if your pillow were really a nice fluffy cloud that you could float away on when you dream?"

"Neat idea," said Bert. "Good night now, Ernie."

"Just imagine," said Ernie. "You'd sail way up high in the sky. Fields would unfold beneath you like a patchwork quilt. Towns below would be tiny. Wouldn't that be something, old buddy?"

"Yes, it would be something, but if you don't mind, Ernie, I'd like to go to sleep now." Bert turned over on his side with his back to Ernie. He tugged his covers more tightly around him.

"What if your knees were mountains? Did you ever think of that, Bert?" asked Ernie.

"No, Ernie," answered Bert. "I never thought of that. Not once."

Ernie bent his knees under the covers. "Look, Bert!" said Ernie. He let his fingers do the walking up over his knees. "Bo-dee-oh-doh! My fingers are hiking up the mountains. What an excellent view! Hee, hee, hee!"

Bert didn't laugh at all. "Okay, Ernie," he said. "Very funny. Could we please get a little sleep now?"

"Anything you say, Bert. But wouldn't it be incredible if there were a huge earthquake?" Ernie shook his knees so it looked like the mountains were trembling. "Rumble, rumble," he said. "*Boom! Bang! Thunder! Lightning!* Oh, no! The mountains are tumbling down. There they go, Bert. Watch, Bert!"

Ernie knocked his knees together and the blankets rippled over them. "Geronimo!" yelled Ernie as his fingers jumped off the crumbling mountains.

"Ernieeee!" groaned Bert.

"Luckily," said Ernie, "there is no earthquake and there are no mountains, just my good old tired knees! Yep, Bert, it sure is nice to get into bed after a long day. Good night, old buddy. Sleep tight!" Ernie yawned and snuggled down under his covers. Soon he was snoring soundly.

Bert couldn't sleep. He sat up and peeked over at Ernie to make sure his friend was truly asleep. Then Bert bent his knees like Ernie so they looked like mountains. Bert walked his fingers up the mountains. At the top of the mountains his fingers paused. "Good night, knees!" said Bert. Then he walked his fingers step-by-step down the mountain and over the covers. Bert began to relax. He hummed, "Bo-dee-oh-doh!" His pillow felt soft as a cloud. "Good night, pillow!" whispered Bert. Then he drifted off into a deep, sweet sleep.